A Look at DOGS

Written by Monica Halpern

STECK-VAUGHN
COMPANY
ELEMENTARY • SECONDARY • ADULT • LIBRARY

D1511787

Contents

What Dogs Are Like

    Dogs can be just about any shape or size. Some are so tall that they can rest their head on a kitchen table. Others are so small that they can fit in a cereal bowl. Some have hair so long it touches the floor. And others have no hair at all.

Most people enjoy having a dog for a pet. Dogs are usually friendly. They like to be petted and to play games. Most dogs are very **loyal** to their owners. Dogs would do just about anything to please them.

Dogs Are Workers

Dogs can be trained to do many special jobs. Some are **watchdogs** or helpers on farms. Others help people who cannot see or hear. Some learn to do tricks that make people laugh. But most dogs just have the job of being a pet.

Dogs can help people. They can let us know when someone is hurt or in danger. Dogs have even rescued their owners in **emergencies.**

Some dogs help firefighters rescue people and animals from dangerous fires. Many firefighters choose Dalmatians to help them.

Many dogs **protect** their owners when they sense danger. Some may even attack or bite. Police dogs are good at protecting people. Most police dogs are German shepherds. They help the police by sniffing out danger.

Seeing eye dogs and hearing dogs do very important jobs. Seeing eye dogs help people who cannot see. Hearing dogs help people who cannot hear. They are trained to go everywhere with their owners.

These dogs go to a special school to learn their jobs. A seeing eye dog wears a **harness** that its owner holds. A hearing dog wears a bright yellow or orange collar for its owner to see.

Dogs also help farmers do their jobs. Farmers often raise animals, such as cows, chickens, goats, and sheep. Farm dogs often help farmers take care of the animals. Border collies can **herd** sheep from one place to another.

Dogs that are very large and strong can do a good job of moving things for people. In snowy places, teams of dogs pull sleds over the ice.

Some dogs pull sleds in races. Huskies do best at this job. They work together as a team to move sleds as fast as possible. These dogs have thick coats to keep warm and strong legs to pull sleds.

The job of **tracking** is one that bloodhounds do well. They use their sense of smell to find missing things or missing people. First, they sniff something so they know the **scent** they need to find. Then these dogs track that scent. They help firefighters and police.

Some dogs have the job of doing tricks for people. These dogs can be trained by their owners to do special moves. They listen carefully to their owners so they know what to do. They can perform in movies or on television.

Dogs Are Friends

Dogs can do many different kinds of jobs. One of the most important jobs is being a friend to someone.

Dogs will let people know they are friendly by wagging their tails, barking, or giving kisses. People can let dogs know they are friendly, too. People can pet them, give them soft hugs, brush them, give them treats, and talk to them with kind words. How can you be a friend to a dog?

Glossary

emergencies serious problems that need attention right away

harness straps that hold a dog's body

herd to gather a group of animals together

loyal being a good friend

protect to keep from harm

scent a smell

tracking following footprints or scents

watchdogs dogs trained to guard